DEIRDRE

A CELTIC LEGEND

Marian F. McNamara
840 University Avenue
Palo Alto Ca 94301
June 12, 1998

DEIRDRE

A CELTIC LEGEND

RELATED BY DAVID GUARD
ILLUSTRATIONS BY GRETCHEN GUARD

Celestial Arts

Published by CELESTIAL ARTS, 231 Adrian Road,
Millbrae, California 94030

First printing: May, 1977
Manufactured in the United States of America

Library of Congress Cataloging in Publication Data

Guard, David, 1934-
Children of exile.

1. Deirdre—Legends. I. Guard, Gretchen, 1937-
II. Title.
PZ4.G897Ch [PS3557.U19] 813'.5'4 77-23492
ISBN 0-89087-201-5

1 2 3 4 5 6 7 8 — 82 81 80 79 78 77

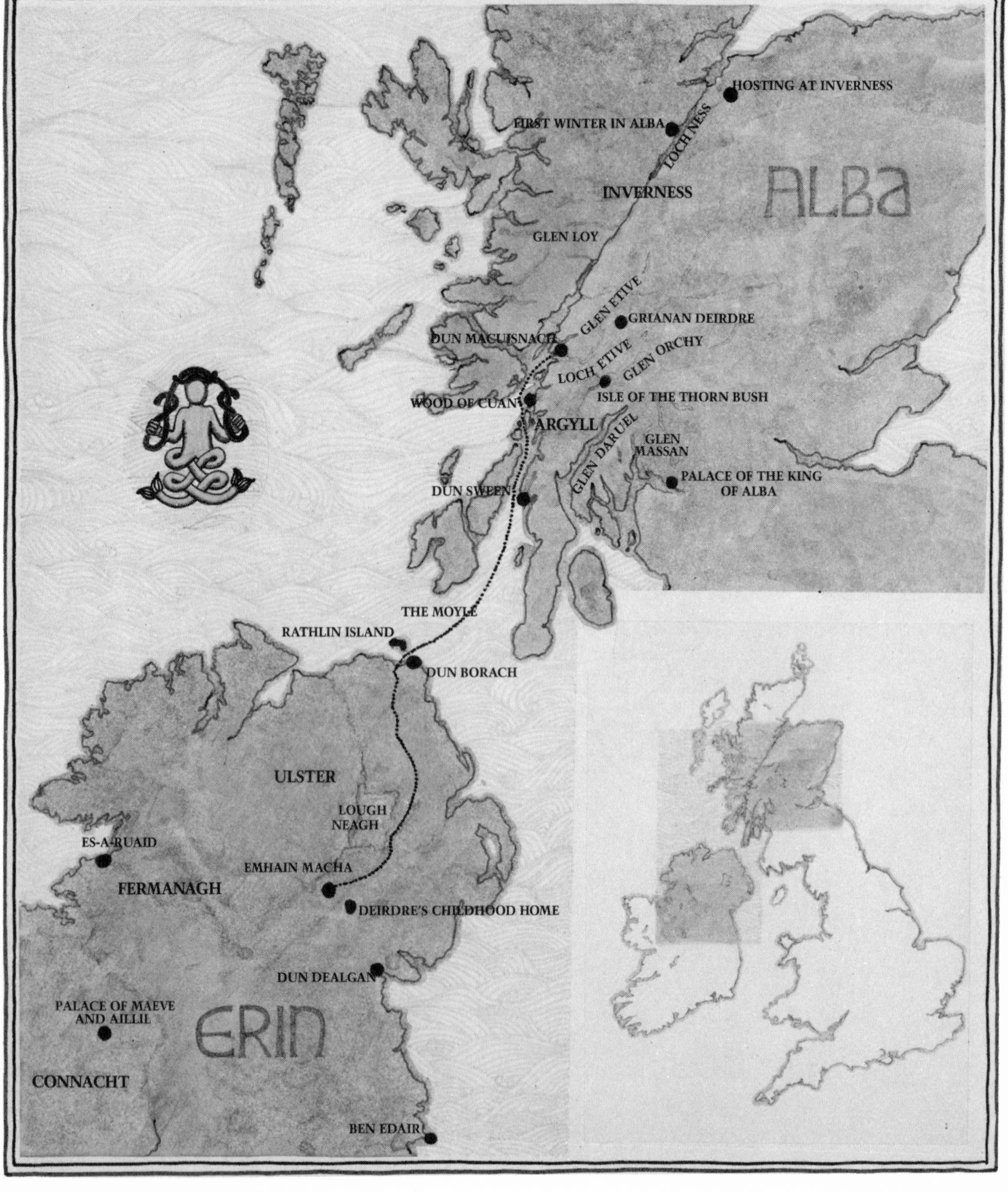

HOSTING AT INVERNESS
FIRST WINTER IN ALBA
LOCH NESS
INVERNESS
ALBA
GLEN LOY
GLEN ETIVE
GRIANAN DEIRDRE
DUN MACUISNACH
LOCH ETIVE
GLEN ORCHY
ISLE OF THE THORN BUSH
WOOD OF CUAN
ARGYLL
GLEN DARUEL
GLEN MASSAN
PALACE OF THE KING OF ALBA
DUN SWEEN
THE MOYLE
RATHLIN ISLAND
DUN BORACH
ULSTER
LOUGH NEAGH
ES-A-RUAID
EMHAIN MACHA
FERMANAGH
DEIRDRE'S CHILDHOOD HOME
DUN DEALGAN
PALACE OF MAEVE AND AILLIL
ERIN
CONNACHT
BEN EDAIR

INTRODUCTION

In the province of Ulster, Northern Ireland, stands the ancient city of Armagh (arMAH) whose name means "the height of Macha" (MAha). Two miles west of this city, around the year 300 BC, the warrior queen Macha compelled her captives taken in battle to build the great hilltop fortress of Emhain Macha (EVan MAha) which served for the next six hundred years as the center of government for Ulster.

Emhain Macha was the headquarters of the Knights of the Red Branch, a band of hardy warriors whose deeds are recorded in the oldest prose epic known to Western literature, *The Cattle Raid of Cooley (Tain Bo Cuailgne)* and in a number of shorter stories, known collectively as the *Tales of the Red Branch.*

The Exile of the Children of Uisnach (WISHna), also known as the story of *Deirdre* (DAREdra) appears most often as a prelude to the main epic, portraying events in Ulster and the highland districts of Scotland during the early years of the first century.

Concobar macNessa, high king of Ulster, chief of the Red Branch, renowned through all of Erin and the lands beyond, went to enjoy a feast in the house of Fedlimid macDall, who was his harper and storyteller.

Lighthearted and merry were the king and the people. Meat and winehorns went round as they listened to the melody of the poets' voices, the ancient tales of the sages and the

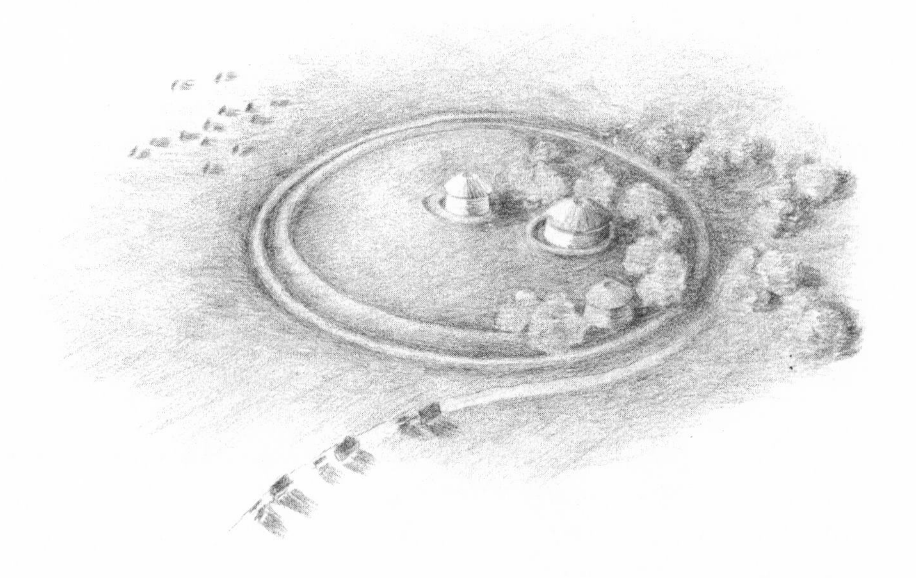

familiar chants of those who read the images written on flags and books, and the prophecies of those who numbered the moon and stars. The rush lights sparkled far and wide, and everyone, wholly given over to the festivity, raised a gigantic uproar. Fedlimid the harper also rejoiced, even though his wife was full with child and expecting that very day or the next, and he wished the king might have come to him at some other time. But now it was the feast of Samhain, the harvest night when past and future are revealed in the showers of falling stars, and it fell to the king's harper to play the host at this turn of the season.

In the midst of the merriment King Concobar noticed that Cathbad, the silver-haired druid who accompanied him, seemed to be staring into the otherworld. The druid turned to Concobar saying, "Weary as I am with my burdens of age and sorrow, did I not beg that I might come with you to this festival? Not that I suddenly have developed an appetite for harping and singing, for I care more to listen to the wind through the grasses or to the sighing upon the hill than to any music of war or love . . ." But before the druid could say more, there arose a shrill and frightened scream which sounded like the cry of a wounded animal in its agony. A sudden fear swept through the company silencing everything but the echo of that scream; then at once every man was on his feet with weapons drawn.

"Do not stir," commanded the king. "No one move until we know what caused that noise." Quickly it was discovered that Elva, the wife of the harper, had been crossing the room when the unborn child in her womb had shrieked so as to be heard by everyone in the house.

Cathbad the druid, who had eaten the hazelnuts of knowledge, who was the interpreter of dreams and omens, stood up directly and, taking his staff of rowan ash in his left hand, went out into the night to pace in slow sunwise circles around the borders of the homestead, carefully observing the clouds of the air, the positions of the stars, the age of the moon, all the while repeating the chant of prophecy. Under

the power of this chant, the veil that hides the future was lifted before his mind, and in a sacred frenzy the druid returned to the room of the women, with the king and his warriors following respectfully.

At Elva's bedside the druid bent low and began his interpretation: "Woman, this is no common child you are carrying. Within the cradle of your womb cries a girl child with curling gold hair and gentle green eyes of great beauty. Her mouth is a crimson fruit with a tongue full of sounds sweeter than the wild music of the hills. It is of her that I speak, this tender fawn in all her loveliness." Then Cathbad placed his hand over the woman's belly, and the child stormed beneath his touch. "True it is a daughter, and her name shall be Deirdre. But out of her beauty will arise a sharp sword to split apart the Tree of Ulster."

Then the druid spoke directly to the unborn child. . . "Oh Deirdre, when you are a famous beauty the Ulstermen will suffer in your time. Kings will seek to marry you, and because of this there will be disaster. I see the Red Branch divided against itself and many of our heroes flying across the boundary into exile. I see strife and warfare among the chariot warriors of Ulster. I see the flames of Emhain Macha starting upward in the dark night, and because of you there will be weasels and wildcats crying on a lonely wall where once there were queens and armies and red gold. There will be a story told of a ruined city and a raving king and a woman who will be young forever!"

The company remained stunned and silent for a few moments. "Kill the child!" cried one of the warriors. Another shouted, "Have her slain at birth!" "Better that than the destruction of us all!" "What says the king to this?"

Concobar had withdrawn from the argument, preferring to weigh the matter privately. While the others were frightened by the prophecy, he was intrigued by it. His respect for the druid's wisdom was great, but his curiosity about this extraordinary beauty was greater still. At length he began, "I will speak first to Fedlimid, my harper and true friend. It is not a good thing to witness the death of one's own child, and it is not right for me or any of my people to bring the pain of death to the house of a friend." There was a storm of protest, but the king continued, "Listen to me, heroes of the Red Branch, and understand that while I believe the prophecies and foretelling of our druid, I will never agree to sacrifice this innocent child in return for an easier fate. Let us accept the prophecy nobly and without disrupting our lawful order. I will take the child and raise her in a secluded place, and when she is grown I will marry her myself. As my ward and then as my wife she will cause no rivalry nor bitterness among our people; therefore she can bring no harm to Ulster. In this way the prophecy will be fulfilled yet be defeated. I free you of all fear for upon me alone is the burden of this prophecy from now forward. That is my word."

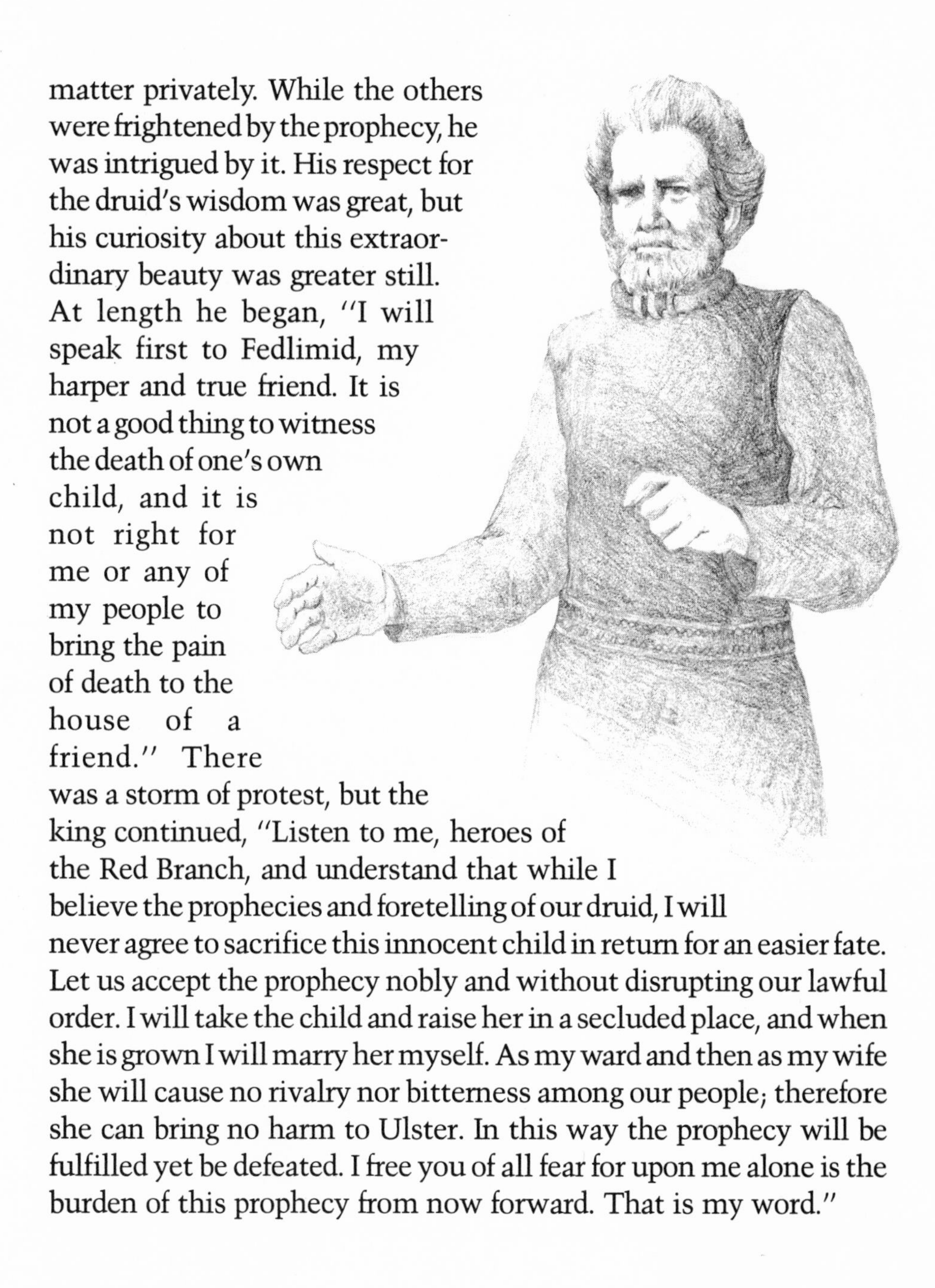

Then the king asked Cathbad the druid if there was anything further to the prophecy, and Cathbad said very quietly, "There is one law. That which has to come cannot be seen until it already is upon us."

Just then loud chanting voices of the women were heard, crying that a child was born to Elva, and that it was a daughter, beautiful and strong. As none of the men of Ulster was so hardy as to turn the king from his purpose, the life of the girl was spared. The rest of that night was spent in peace, and when the days of the feast were done, the king left the house of Fedlimid and returned with his own people to the palace at Emhain Macha, taking with him the infant Deirdre.

Cathbad the druid gave warning that before a year and a day were gone, the king must arrange to have the baby hidden away where no eye would see her and no ear would hear her. So upon the first fine morning of spring, Concobar took his most trusted men with him high up into the royal forest and had them build a small house in a hilltop hollow, a place surrounded by apple trees. When the dwelling was done, the king had them build a high, thick wall of stone to enclose the orchard on all sides so the place was like a concealed fortress. And a prohibition was put on this part of the forest that none might hunt or stray near without the king's permission, and the ban was absolute. Death would be the fate of the man found under these branches.

Only three people would be allowed within the walls to provide for Deirdre: her foster father; the nursing woman who was his wife; and the governess named Levarcham. Levarcham was a handsome and intelligent young woman who had been raised as a chronicler and storyteller in the household of Concobar, and was trusted by the king beyond all others.

While Deirdre was still in her first year, Levarcham took her away to their new home for the years of her childhood, where she was to be given excessive luxury of meat and milk to increase her stature and hasten her ripeness so that she would be sooner marriageable to Concobar.

Deirdre grew lithe and fair as the sapling, and straight and clean as the young moorland rush. Her motions were those of the swan on the wave or the deer on the hill. And Levarcham taught her every knowledge and skill she herself possessed, until the girl knew the ways of every herb and flower, every bird and insect, and every bright star in the heavens. She and Levarcham loved each other like mother and daughter, so that Levarcham gradually relaxed the severity of her confinement, allowing Deirdre to wander the forested hillsides outside the high wall, to gather flowers and listen to the humming of woodland life.

As Deirdre grew, the Province of Ulster prospered, so that the palace at Emhain Macha became famous throughout every province of the Western world for its might and splendor and for the heroic knights of the Red Branch who defended the kingdom of Concobar macNessa against every enemy.

From the time Deirdre was a baby the king saw little of her, only twice in the year. First at Belteine, the festival of bonfires, in the month of the rowan tree; and again at Samhain, the festival of summerend in the month of ivy. The Druid permitted these visits only until Deirdre's seventh year, and now seven more years had gone since the king had taken delight in her loveliness. But he had word of her from Levarcham who, in going and coming, had only one thing to say, that Deirdre was as enchanting as the rising moon and as radiant as the setting sun. The rumor of her perfect beauty spread throughout the land, yet no one ventured into the mountain wilderness where Deirdre was hidden.

In her fifteenth year when Levarcham told the king that Deirdre grew fairer and fairer so that even the wild creatures of the woods rejoiced in her, he announced to his household that when the time of the first greening was over, when the wild rose runs like a flame through the land, he would have Deirdre for his bride and consort. On hearing of this, Deirdre was overcome with sadness. She lost all desire for food; her sleep was restless and filled with visions. To Levarcham it seemed her very spirit had deserted her as she spent her days of melancholy sitting by the window listlessly embroidering a cloth. Each earlier twilight brought a colder wind. All too soon the snows came back from the north and settled upon the forest.

One cold bright morning, her foster father was skinning a calf on the snow outside to cook for dinner. While she looked, a raven came gliding over the snow to the slain calf and began drinking its bright blood. "I think," said Deirdre, "that the man I marry will have those three colors about him: His hair black like the raven's, his face as fair as the snow, with cheeks as red as that blood. I saw such a young man in my dream last night, but I know not where he is, nor whether he exists at all."

"I am amazed you should be telling me your dream in just this way," said Levarcham, "for down in Emhain Macha they use those very words in praise of a young champion who is living there. He is among Concobar's knights, and his name is Naisi, of the three sons of Uisnach. You shall have the loyalty and protection of this knight when you are the wife of his king. Come away from your dreaming and turn your thoughts to the happiness which is in store for you."

"The king is so old," said Deirdre, "and my dream is more real to me than anything you say about the King."

"The king is a great man," said Levarcham. "He is very kind and has given you everything. At the beginning, he saved your very life!"

"Oh mother," cried Deirdre, "if you want me to go on living, go to Naisi of my dream and ask him to come and find me in the forest outside the wall."

"Child, you cannot know the danger in what you ask. If your foster parents hear of it, they are bound to tell the king."

Deirdre made no answer, but remained sad and silent throughout the last winter of her childhood, her eyes often filling with tears at the memory of her dream. Levarcham grieved for her. She worried that Deirdre's heart would break if she and Naisi were not allowed to meet, and she feared Concobar's furious vengeance if such a thing were discovered. After many fretful days, because she loved Deirdre more than anything in the world, she made her difficult way down to the encampment at Emhain Macha to seek out the three warrior sons

of Uisnach. There she found them engaged in feats and contests on the green in front of the palace. She was not disappointed with Naisi for he was the most beautiful of the brothers with the colors of the girl's dream indeed upon him. Putting aside her worst fears for their safety, Levarcham told him of the young girl and her dreams.

"Deirdre! I remember that name from some tale of my childhood," said Naisi.

"Then come soon and hunt deer in the solitudes north of the forest," said Levarcham, "and there in some glen or on the hillside you may find her and none will know of it. Such wilderness is open to the flight of the owl as well as the soaring hawk."

So it was told. Levarcham and Naisi parted with a wave, and she made her journey back to Deirdre. Late the next day, Levarcham and Deirdre ventured outside the wall as they often did, to wander the lonely hillside and collect herbs and flowers. The forest was warm with the new life of spring.

"There is a strange thing," Deirdre said, "for just now I heard the cry of the jay, but it was the one he gives in alder month, at the nesting time. And now listen! That was the bark of the hill fox, but it was the one he gives in his own mating season, many months ago!"

"Hush," said Levarcham, "and look!"

They saw three young men coming up the glen together, and Deirdre looked at them in wonder. As they drew nearer she knew they were the sons of Uisnach, and this was Naisi, the tallest and handsomest of the three. The brothers passed by without turning their eyes at all toward the watching women. They were singing as they went and their song was pure enchantment to Deirdre and Levarcham, but at the same time the shadows were lengthening in the wood and the sons of Uisnach were widening the distance between them. Deirdre hugged Levarcham hurriedly, gathered her skirts and ran after them.

Naisi left the chase of the deer and turned to make his way through the green glooms of the royal forest. In a clearing under a high ceiling of branches, Deirdre slipped out near him in passing, pretending not to notice him.

"Oh, that is a fine heifer going by," Naisi laughed.

"And why not?" said Deirdre. "The heifers just keep growing where there are no bulls."

"But you have the bull of the province all to yourself," said Naisi. "I have heard he loves you as some old miser loves the dragon stone he hides among the cobwebs near the roof."

"All of that is true," she said. "It was against the wishes of the king that I've come out of my house without my mother. I have spent all my life behind the walls of the dreary fortress where he has me locked away. At the new moon they are coming to take me down to his palace. The bird will be freed from the fowler's net only to be forced into the wicker cage.

"Forgive me for speaking this way, Naisi, but I would love you as in days of old, when Dectera the queen loved the green harper, went away with him and was seen no more by her own people."

"Ah but you couldn't Deirdre! Have you forgotten the druid's prophecy?"

"Are you rejecting me then?"

"That I am," said Naisi.

She rushed at him and caught him by the ears. "Two ears of shame and mockery if you don't take me with you!"

"Woman, leave me alone!" cried Naisi helplessly, laughing and going round and round with her.

"You will do it," she said. "You must!"

Prying loose her hands and taking them firmly in his own he said, "Now surely, Deirdre, there is no burly warrior of the Red Branch can match your courage, but it may be that you speak so freely from knowing so little of what might happen."

"What bold words from the proud son of a proud family!" she said scornfully.

Naisi tried to hide a smile. She looked at him as though seeing him for the first time, and before more could be said, she put her mouth on his and with the confusion that went through them, a blaze of red fire came upon her in an instant, and just as quickly faded away. Naisi had never held a woman so beautiful in his life, and from that moment he gave to Deirdre the love he never gave to another living thing. He stepped away from her a little and spoke to her evenly.

"There is still time, Deirdre. For your own sake will you go back to your house and stay there until the king calls for you?"

Looking at him steadily she said, "I value this one perfect day with you, Naisi, more than a lifetime with Concobar." Then she smiled brightly and slipped her arm in his saying "Besides, we're young, and that's the time to see the world. We can always come back!"

They hurried down the wooded slope first walking, then running, in search of his brothers. Before long they came to the friendly hounds who led them to the clearing where the brothers were hunting. Ainlle and Ardan greeted Deirdre and made her welcome, but they said, "There will be trouble because of this. Is she not the girl who is fated to destroy Ulster? However we'll not be disgraced as long as we stay together. There is not a king in Erin who would not make us welcome."

With all speed they summoned those of their following who were under the sword-bond to put together food and clothing, and they went away that night, with three times fifty men, three times fifty women and the same of greyhounds and menials, with Deirdre in their midst, mingling with the rest. Thus it was, the Clanna Uisnach deserted the house of Concobar macNessa, going over the border into exile.

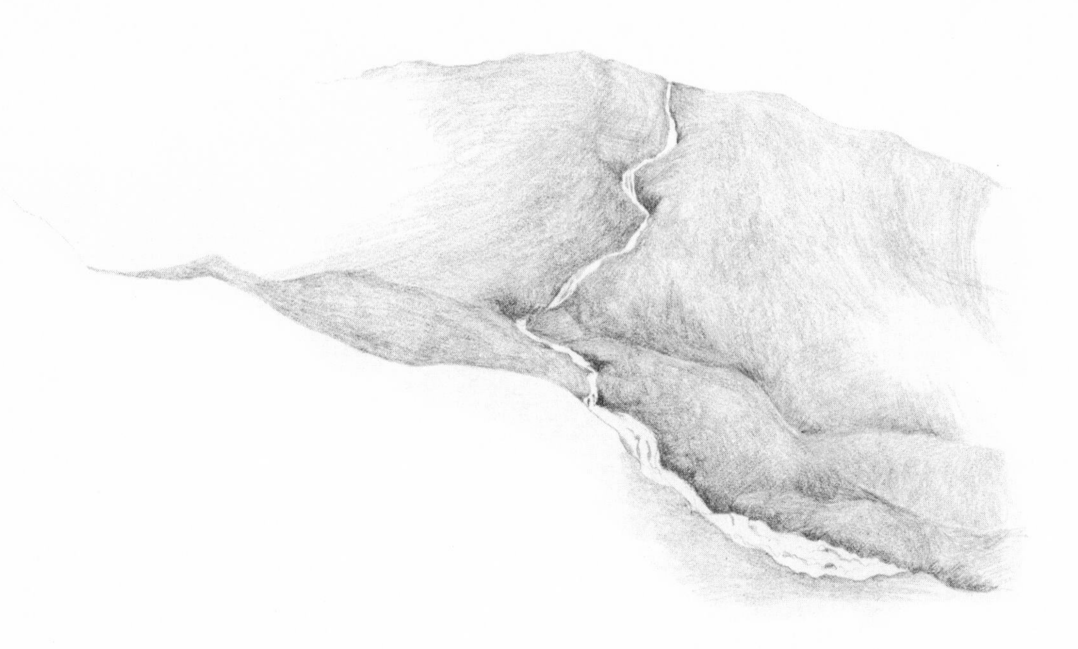

For a long time they wandered about Erin in homage to this man or that. In this way, it is said, they journeyed southwestward from Es-Ruaid in Donegal, and later northeastward to Ben Etair. Where they woke in the morning they dared not sleep that night, so unrelenting was the pursuit of Concobar's agents, who plotted their ambush and betrayal at every turn.

As Deirdre and the brothers sat by their open fire one night, they talked about the risks of staying in Erin and of the danger to the whole clan. They agreed they must leave their homeland at once and go to Alba over the sea. Naisi, Ainlle and Ardan had been trained there as young boys to hunt and fight, and they knew the mountains and glens

of Alba nearly as well as their own land. There they hoped to find plenty of wild game to hunt, freedom to roam the hills and valleys, and safety from Concobar's wiles and snares.

So they sailed over the sea to the land of Alba, taking only a few of their clan with them, and there took refuge at last upon the wild and lonely shores of the Black Loch, Loch Ness.

At first they made their living by hunting upon the mountain, but when this failed them they took to stealing the cattle of the men of Alba, who gathered together to put an end to them in a single day. Naisi and his brothers went to the soldiers of the king of Alba and offered their service as warriors in exchange for the king's protection. The king agreed to this proposal and readily accepted the three sons of Uisnach among his own people.

On the green below the stronghold of the king they set up their huts in the night. Because of Deirdre's great beauty, they placed the huts so that none could see her from outside, for fear there might be bloodshed on her account. But as it happened, the king's steward came looking around among their huts very early one morning and saw them asleep side by side. He hurried back to awaken the king and tell him, "Until today there never has been a woman who would make you a fitting wife, but I have just seen a woman worthy of the king of the Western world. She is living with Naisi, son of Uisnach. If something should happen to Naisi, you would have her for yourself.

"Go to her," said the king of Alba, "while the sons of Uisnach are hunting, and tell her to come to me."

The steward brought her the king's message, not once but three times. Each time, Deirdre refused the king, and what the steward would tell her by day, she related to her husband by night. Since she couldn't be persuaded, the sons of Uisnach were ordered into every risk and difficulty. But they were steadfast in every battle. Standing with their three backs together, their parrying and defense would bring them back safe again to Deirdre, and all the king's efforts came to nothing. Angered by his last failure he silently gathered his own men to kill the brothers.

"I am afraid," Deirdre said to Naisi, "if we do not leave this place tonight we will be dead here tomorrow."

So they fled the stronghold of the king of Alba, and for several days travelled on foot northwestward to the shores of Loch Etive, where they took up their living again by hunting and fishing. As they

were left in peace, they settled in the upper glen by a waterfall and made a house of long-stalked ferns and red clay from the pools, and they lined the inside with the down feathers of birds. Here they could catch the salmon of the stream from their own door and the deer of the hills from their window. And they named the place Granian Deirdre, which means Deirdre's sunny home.

After a time the mountain people in the lands to the northeast offered their loyalty to the sons of Uisnach in return for the protection of these skillful warriors, and many of their fellow clansmen travelled across the sea from Erin to join them in exile. They became as chiefs over Argyll, leading the tribes of the great glen to the hosting of Inverness. In summer they climbed to the heights overlooking Loch

Ness, but before the first frost they would return to the Bay of Selma on the coast, to warm themselves within the fire-glazed walls of their winter stronghold high on the ridge facing Erin. They named this place Dun macUisnach, the fortress of the sons of Uisnach.

Often they wandered far on foot, over the coast lands and through the glens. And when it was pleasant to be on the water, they sailed to the south and then eastward among the sea lochs and narrow kyles. And in these days Deirdre thought that in all the world there could be none so happy as themselves.

In the seventh year of exile, as the month-long festival of Lugnasa was beginning, King Concobar hosted a grand banquet in smooth delightful Emhain Macha for all the worthies of the province of Ulster. Great portions of meat and wine were served to each guest until all were merry and joyous. At the pleasure of the king, the men of music and playing and knowledge arose to recite lays and songs and chants, to the accompaniment of sweet resounding harp-

strings. And these are the names of some of the poets who were in Emhain Macha at that time: Cathbad the druid, son of Congal Flatnose, son of Rudraighe; and Genan Brightcheek, son of Cathbad; and Genan Blackknee, also son of Cathbad; and Ferchertne, the son of Angus Redmouth. There was Sencha, son of the king of Connacht, and many other poets as well. In all there were three hundred and sixty-five guests under Concobar's roof that night.

At the height of the festivities Concobar stood up and raised his voice above the merry din so that all were hushed in a moment. "I want to know," he said, "have you ever seen a better house than this house of Emhain Macha? Or any hearth better than my hearth?"

"Truly we have not," answered one and all.

"If that is so," said Concobar, "do you know of anything at all that is wanting here?"

"We know of nothing," they answered.

Then the king said, "But I know of a great want which we have, namely that some of our greatest people are not among us tonight. I speak of the three torches of the Gael: Naisi, Ainlle and Ardan, the sons of Uisnach, who was the son of Congal, who was the son of Rudraighe, and by this branch, brothers of my own blood. Now I declare that it is not fitting that these three heroes be forever condemned to exile, and this only on account of a woman. Had they stayed in Ulster, the sons of Uisnach might be leading my troops today. By the strength of their arms they have gained a district and a half in Alba! If we had these champions at home once again, the Red Branch would be united and at full strength. We might well defend this kingdom during the dark days which the druid has foretold."

"If we had dared," said one after another of the king's guests, "we would have said it and more. The province of Ulster would be equal to any other in Erin if there were none of the Red Branch in it but those three together, for they are like lions in hardness and bravery. It would be better to welcome them and feed them and not to kill them, and for them to come home to their own land, rather than to have them fall at the hands of foreigners."

"Seeing that we are all agreed," said Concobar, "it is time to send someone over to Alba with the message that the king has pardoned the sons of Uisnach and wishes to welcome them home."

"Who will go with that message?" they asked.

"By the laws of exile," said Concobar, "only the word of a king is strong enough to guarantee the safe return of these men. They have been outlaws for years, with a high price on their heads."

"I can think of no more fitting messenger of our good intentions than the man here by my side, who was the king of Ulster before me: Fergus macRoigh."

And so before the cheering assembly, a surprised Fergus found himself pledging to safeguard the return of the sons of Uisnach from Alba.

Much later that night, King Concobar summoned his own man, Beoragh, whose fortress on the north coast overlooked the shortest waterway to Alba. "Do you have a feast laid out for me?" asked the king. "That I have," said Beoragh, "and though it is ready for you, it is not possible to carry it to you here in Emhain Macha."

"Don't worry," laughed the king, "you are to set a royal ale-feast in honor of Fergus macRoigh when he returns with the sons of Uisnach. Fergus must preside over the celebration until I myself

arrive. Meanwhile, send the sons of Uisnach to me, wherever I may be at the time. According to our laws, returning exiles may take no food in Erin but that of my own table first. Your efforts will be more than generously rewarded, you may be certain."

Beoragh agreed to these arrangements, saying he was well prepared at all times to receive guests or to repel invaders.

Early next morning the former king of Ulster, Fergus macRoigh, set out for the northern coast, taking with him his two sons, Illand Fairheaded and Buinne Roughred, and the man called Cullen who carried Fergus's shield. It was a fair voyage they made in the black royal galleys and a favoring wind carried them swiftly past the isles and headlands of Alba.

Plying northward past the mouth of Loch Etive, they entered the Bay of Selma and soon caught sight of the ridge mound rising abruptly from the beach, crowned by a gleaming dark fortress, sharply outlined against the ivy clad heights beyond. To every passing mariner it was the landmark known as Dun macUisnach, the stronghold of the sons of Uisnach.

Fergus sent up his mighty hunting call in the harbor. At this moment the sons of Uisnach were some distance from their fortress, out of sight and almost beyond earshot. The three brothers had put up wicker hunting booths in the forest near the shoreline. And the booth in which their food was prepared they did not eat, and the booth in which they ate they did not sleep. In the last booth Deirdre and Naisi had a chess board between them and were advancing the men upon it. Naisi could hear the sound of Fergus's call coming through the shoreline trees, and said, "That is a call we used to hear in Erin."

"It is not," said Deirdre. "It was the cry of a man of these waters."

Fergus gave another mighty roar, and Naisi said, "Again! That is an Irish shout!"

"Indeed it was not," she said. "Let's go on playing. The moment I gain advantage, you begin to welcome distractions! Give me my chance at this game!"

But when a third call was heard, nearer than ever, Naisi leapt to his feet. "Now that was Fergus!" And he sent Ardan running down to the water's edge to welcome the voyagers.

"It may be that Concobar is dead," said Naisi.

Then Deirdre confessed that she had known from the first shout that it was Fergus. "I had a vision in a dream last night," she said. "Three ravens came flying to us over the sea from Emhain Macha, and they brought three drops of honey in their beaks. These honey drops they left with us, and took away with them three drops of blood."

"What meaning do you give your dream?" asked Naisi.

"It means Fergus comes to us from Concobar with honey sweet offers of peace. The three drops of blood are Ainlle and Ardan and yourself whom Concobar would flatter and lure into his trap."

As Ardan ran out upon the beach he quickly recognized Fergus and his two sons. These were friends from earliest boyhood, and he cried out to them in affectionate welcome and gave them three kisses right loyally. He brought them to the lodges where Naisi and Deirdre and Ainlle gave them another warm welcome and asked them news of Erin and of Ulster.

"The best news," said Fergus, "is that King Concobar is preparing a great banquet for his friends and kinsmen throughout Erin and he has vowed by the earth beneath him, by the sky above and by the power of the sun that he will not have a night of rest nor a day of peace until the children of Uisnach return to the land of their home and the country of their inheritance. I have come over as a guarantee for your safety, to see you honorably restored to your places in the Red Branch. Surely it is good to end a feud and put away the sword and spear."

"And surely Concobar macNessa forgets," said Deirdre, "that Naisi is now overlord of a land larger than all of Ulster. The world's turned upside down when the king of an island goes as the forgiven guest of the lord of a rock."

"Ah, but one's own country is better loved than any other," said Fergus. "Life is sad when a man wakes in the morning and finds himself too long away from home."

"That is truth to me," said Naisi. "Erin still owns my heart, even though we have made a good life here."

"Deirdre," Naisi said, "in my flight I have brought with me many whose true wish is to see home again, while you are a fixed star by my side, no matter where we go. Many a maiden sighs for the clansman who may never return. There is also the heavy burden of disgrace upon our name, because I fled and did not face the king. Shall I swear to keep my comrades in exile, and let the shame of cowardice rest on the head of their clan?"

"We are of two lands," said Ardan, "still we look upon ourselves as of the Red Branch first and foremost."

"It is harmless for you to go with me," said Fergus.

Fergus gave his vow in the presence of his weapons that if any attempt be made upon the lives of the children of Uisnach, he and his sons would leave no guilty head on its shoulders. And Naisi and his brothers in turn agreed that they would not eat food in Erin until they had eaten from Concobar's table first.

The decision to return to Ulster was made without Deirdre's consent and as they wore away that night she shed tears and related dreams and omens, giving Naisi little rest. He said to her, "When we give or take a word, we pledge more than our own one life, but the lives of our clansmen as well. None would be alive today were there not this means of putting away past grievances."

When Deirdre arose next morning, she walked down to the edge of the water and there saw Naisi and Fergus in a galley together, each preparing to man an oar. Many of their people also were there, stowing their belongings and settling into the ships. She knew they would not be persuaded to stay, so she climbed the steep plank and took a place at the rail on a pile of skins and robes.

All day and into evening, wind and the work of the rowing men brought them steadily southwestward across the cold expanse of the Moyle. Falling far behind them was Loch Etive of the storms, the land of the fresh forest trees. Deirdre took her harp and sat back among the deerskins in the stern of the galley and began to sing a sorrowful farewell to Alba. There the hands of all the mariners were relaxed and every oar suspended, for the sadness of her song pierced the starry night and dissolved every heart:

Beloved is that land to the east,
Alba with its bright harbors and pleasing green slopes.
I would not have come away from it
Except to be with Naisi.

Dear to me are Dun Fhada and Dun Fionn;
Well remembered, the stronghold above them.
Dear to me is the Isle of the Thornbush.
Dear to me Dun Sween.

Glen Etive my home;
It was there we raised our first house.
Lovely its wood in the smile of the early morning;
A cattlefold of the sun is Glen Etive.

Wood of Cuan, Caill Cuan
Where Ainlle would go;
Short we thought the time, Naisi and I
Upon the margins of its streams and waterfalls.

Glen Massan;
Tall its wild garlic, bright are its stalks.
We would enjoy a rocking sleep
In the wooded river mouth of Massan.

Glen Orchy;
Over the straight glen rises its smooth ridge.
My love would waken the woods there with his song
Far below the motionless wings of a golden eagle.

The vale of Loigh, Glen Loy;
We would sleep on soft ferns beneath its shapely rock.
Fish and venison and badger's fat,
That was my portion in Glen Loy.

Glen Daruel, glen of the two roes;
Happy the child who is its native.
Sweet the note of the cuckoo from the hazel bough
On the high cliff over Glen Daruel.

Dear to me is Draighen over the resounding shore;
Dear to me its crystal waters over the speckled sand.
I would never have come away from it at all
But that I came with Naisi.

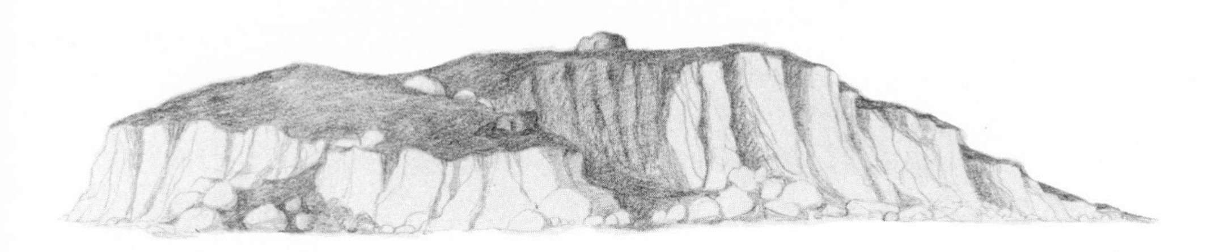

They rowed on in silence until dawn when at last they could see the sunrise reflecting from chalk cliffs over their landing bay in Ulster. They beached their galleys on the wide white sands near Beoragh's sea mountain fortress, and Beoragh ran down to take their hands on landing, calling, "Welcome, Fergus! Push the plank to shore. Descend, fair Deirdre! Sons of Uisnach, hail!"

"I have a three days ale feast laid out for King Concobar," Beoragh said to Fergus, "but he has sent word that you yourself must take his place at the head of the board here tonight. The king cannot leave Emhain Macha now, as he is talking peace with the clans of the west.

Our feast here must be led by someone of the highest royal rank; if not the king himself, then Fergus only. The sons of Uisnach are to proceed to Emhain Macha where Concobar is sure to give them a fine welcome."

This news was a shock to all, but especially to Fergus, whose knightly vows prohibited him from refusing the hospitality of another member of the Red Branch. By these prohibitions he was bound to remain at the feast until it was done. Fergus reddened with anger from footsole to face and he said "It's an evil thing you've done, Beoragh, to hold me under prohibitions, when Concobar has made me give my word to bring the sons of Uisnach to Emhain Macha on the day they should return to Erin. And if I remain feasting in your house, how shall I see that my promise of safety is respected?"

"I hold you to your bonds," said Beoragh, "to stop and use this feast."

And Deirdre said, "Which would you forsake, Fergus, the merrymaking here or the children of Uisnach who have come over on your word alone?"

"I will not be forsaking them," said Fergus, "as I will send my two good sons, Illand Fairheaded and Buinne Roughred with them to Emhain Macha, and they will have my own chariots and horses."

"Enough is his goodness," said Naisi. "Surely we can defend ourselves as we have done always." Then he and Deirdre left the shore with Naisi's brothers, followed by the sons of Fergus, and they began their southward journey in the two-wheeled wicker chariots of the Royal House of Ulster.

Fergus was left dark and sorrowful after them. But he assured himself of one thing: if the five great fifths of Erin were assembled in one council, they would not be able to overturn the pledges of safe conduct he had given. The homeward path of the sons of Uisnach would be cleared of outlaws and fresh horses would await them at every outpost.

Shortly on their way, Deirdre called out to the others, "I will give you a bit of good advice. It is to turn back and take a boat over to Rathlin Island, just off the coast there. One can easily wait until Fergus has done with the feast. That would be a fulfillment of his knightly obligation and a sure lengthening of your own lives."

"How long would any warrior live if his courage abandoned him so quickly?" asked Naisi. "Where would we stand with the Order of the Red Branch if it became known we could not face our own homecoming?"

"So we are to blunder forward," she said, "upon the worthless word of Fergus, who has sold his honor for ale. How sad I am for you, beautiful children of Uisnach, to have come so far from the rough grasses of Alba. Lifelong will be the sorrow of it."

The charioteers drove relentlessly onward along the smooth eastern shorelands of great Lough Neagh. Rounding the south end of the lake they turned the chariots sunwise, galloping headlong into the familiar land of low rolling hills crowned with druid groves of oak and orchards of apple trees. In the last heat of afternoon they stopped to rest and to harness fresh horses to the shafts.

Deirdre wandered a little way into the glen to rest by the stream, and sleep overcame her there. By the time Naisi found her she was just waking. "Another fearful dream," she said, "and in it I saw each of you without a head, even Illand, the son of Fergus. While Buinne, the other son of Fergus, would not come near to save us!"

"This delightful lady sings of nothing but evil," said Naisi. "Oh may the thin slow lip of her venom be ever turned toward the furious foreigner—if only she would spare her poor husband's ears!"

The chariot track led them over the ridge of the willows, not an hour's journey from the palace, and Deirdre, looking towards the setting sun, cried out in great fear, "Oh Naisi, can you see that cloud in the sky over Emhain Macha, cold and deep crimson, a thin and dreadful cloud like clotted blood? Please let us turn southward through the pass here and go tonight to Dundealgan where Cuchulainn the mighty warsmith lives. We can come back up here tomorrow with the expert Cu at our side."

"Please understand, beloved," said Naisi, "we cannot do as you say. It would be a mark of fear, and there is no fear among us."

Soon they came within sight of the smooth white rock ramparts and roof tops of Emhain Macha, and she gave one last counsel. "I have a sign to show you whether Concobar meditates good or evil. You know well, in Emhain Macha there are three great houses of the king: The Tayta Brec, the hall of the twinkling hoard where the sacred relics and battle trophies are kept; next the palace itself where Concobar lives, and last there is the Inn of the Red Branch. If you are invited to eat and drink in Cocobar's house, then all will be well, for no man would shed the blood of a guest at his own table. But if you are invited to the Inn of the Red Branch, you may be sure the king is bent on treachery."

They said nothing to that, and coming late up the spiral chariot ramp to the house of the king, knocked loudly with the handwood upon the great bronze gate. The doorkeeper learned the names of the travelers and sent a runner to Concobar saying it was the sons of Uisnach who had returned with some of their people, among them Fergus's two sons and Deirdre.

"Well, I did not expect they would come so soon," said Concobar, "though I sent a message for them, I am not quite prepared to receive them yet. As you can see we are full with guests here tonight, in celebration of our new alliance with the western clans." The king then called his stewards and serving men, asking how stood the Inn of Red Branch as to food and drink. They replied that if the seven battalions of Ulster would come into it, they would find enough of every good thing, and as the knights of the Red Branch themselves were far from home this night, the king's most recent guests could have the hostel to themselves.

"If that is so," said Concobar, "make them comfortable there." And the king sent stewards and serving men to attend the sons of Uisnach. Deirdre turned to Naisi and said, "An empty house upon the journey's end? Is that the way a king who means no evil honors a guest?" But she went with them down to the Inn of the Red Branch and as they were entering the hall, Naisi told her, "One trained warrior can defend this lodge against any number of Concobar's household slaves. It would take lightning itself to kindle the stout red timbers of these walls. The narrow entryways allow passage by only one at a time, with no room to ready his weapons."

They were waited on by servants who laid straw and fresh rushes underfoot and brought them generous portions of food and bitter cheering drinks until most of the company were well-satisfied. But Naisi and Deirdre felt little appetite, blaming the weariness of their travel. They rested on one of the high dappled fawnskin couches bordering the circular hall; after a while Naisi brought out the chessboard and they began to play.

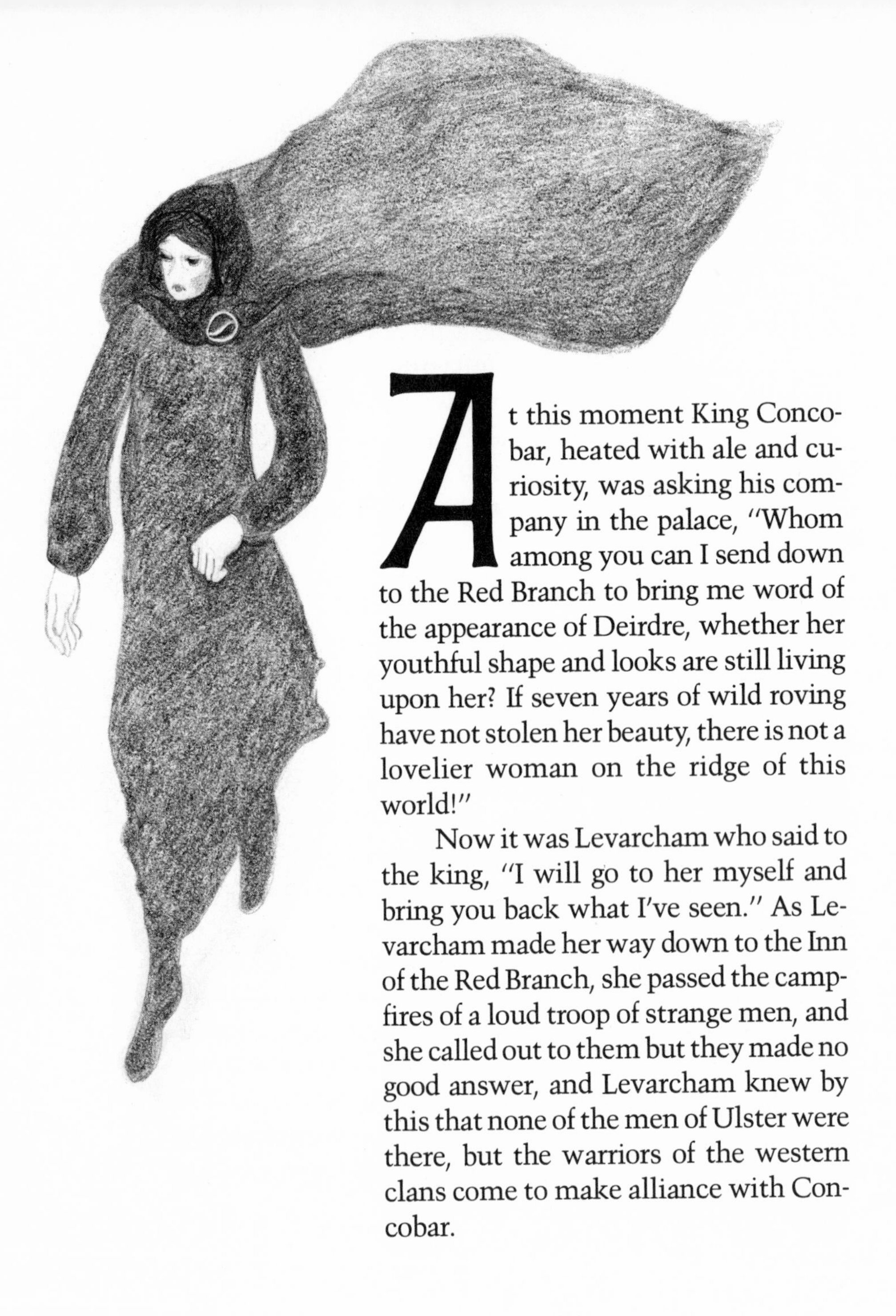

At this moment King Concobar, heated with ale and curiosity, was asking his company in the palace, "Whom among you can I send down to the Red Branch to bring me word of the appearance of Deirdre, whether her youthful shape and looks are still living upon her? If seven years of wild roving have not stolen her beauty, there is not a lovelier woman on the ridge of this world!"

Now it was Levarcham who said to the king, "I will go to her myself and bring you back what I've seen." As Levarcham made her way down to the Inn of the Red Branch, she passed the campfires of a loud troop of strange men, and she called out to them but they made no good answer, and Levarcham knew by this that none of the men of Ulster were there, but the warriors of the western clans come to make alliance with Concobar.

She entered the Inn of the Red Branch to find Naisi and her beloved Deirdre playing upon the polished chessboard, and she gave them loving, fervent kisses. Through her tears Levarcham told them, "My heart is breaking with knowledge of the evil the king plans tonight in Emhain Macha. I was sent here by Concobar to see if Deirdre still has her form and beauty as it was before. The Three Bright Candles of the Gael are to be treacherously attacked and from now until the end of the world we will never be at peace. Your beauty, Deirdre, was once a lingering flame in the imagination of the king, but seeing you now will put the torch to his heart.

"I have passed a company of strange warriors camped behind Emhain Macha this night at the invitation of the king. Their skins have been filled and they are maddened with drink! You must bar every door and window. I will send a messenger for Fergus macRoigh. Be steadfast, sons of Uisnach! You must hold until your father comes, you sons of Fergus; defend your charges manfully and there shall be praise and a blessing for it." Then she made her painful way back to Emhain Macha.

"The situation is both good and bad," Levarcham told the king. "The good news is that the three whose form and make are best, whose motion and throwing of darts, whose action and valor and prowess are first among the men of Erin and Alba, these have returned. With the sons of Uisnach at your side, you will be an irresistible force against the contending tribes of Erin. And the sad thing I must tell you is that the beautiful girl who would have come to Emhain Macha seven years ago is not the haggard woman who comes here tonight. Her youthful shape and splendid features have gone; nothing but tragedy remains."

When Concobar heard this, much of his jealousy subsided for a while. He called for more wine and thought upon Deirdre a second time. "Who can I send to get an honest look?" he asked, but the tone of his voice filled the guests with misgivings of some evil intent, and all remained silent. Concobar called the young Trendorn Dolann, son of Gelban, to him and whispered, "Trendorn, tell me, do you remember who it was who killed your father and three brothers in battle?"

Trendorn replied, "We all know it was Naisi, the son of Uisnach who slew them."

Concobar smiled and said, "Go down and look into the Red Branch and bring a description of the woman who is there with Naisi."

Reluctantly Trendorn left the flickering torchlight of the banquet hall and went outside into the darkness. He moved in a stealthy circle around the Inn of the Red Branch only to find its heavy oak doors barred and its windows shuttered. It would not be easy to approach the sons of Uisnach when they were in such a suspicious mood, Trendorn thought. But at length he discovered a narrow window giving light, climbed up to it from an unyoked chariot which stood near, and peered in to find Deirdre and Naisi playing at chess. Deirdre chanced to look up at that moment and, following his wife's glance, Naisi caught sight of the face at the window. With the spiked and barbed chessman in his hand, Naisi made a fearful successful cast so that it broke the eye in the young man's head. Trendorn dropped down in pain and rage, and ran straightaway to the king to tell him, "I have just seen the loveliest woman in all the world. If it weren't for this unlucky wound I would be there looking at her still!"

Concobar sprang to his feet, a flame of fury in his eyes, and threw back his head in loud and cruel laughter. At this, everyone in the palace knew the king's madness was upon him, the blood-thirst once again upon his sword. "Comrades!" shouted Concobar, "the truth stands out at last. It is now clear that the sons of Uisnach have come here not in peace, but to make rebellion. My messenger returns from them gravely wounded. Chieftains of the west, will you come to the aid of the king of Ulster?"

"That we will!" they replied in a drunken roar.

"Then everyone with me! Surround the outlaws in the house of the Red Branch!"

The soldiers came rushing forth in a mighty surge over the lawn of Emhain Macha and set upon the Red Branch yelling fiercely, brandishing torches and flaming spears. When the sons of Uisnach heard the din they called out through the heavy walls of the lodge, "Who is there outside?"

"It is I, Concobar macNessa, king of Ulster, and let the matter be in darkness to you no longer. My fighters are set round in among the trees. If the woman Deirdre is put out through the door the troops will go away."

Illand Fairheaded shouted in reply, "These people are here under pledges of safe conduct sworn to them by my father, Fergus mac-Roigh!"

"By the laws of my own conscience," replied the king, "it is a greater shame upon yourselves and the sons of Uisnach that my wife is in there with them."

"That is true," said Deirdre quietly, "and Fergus has kept you in a dream, but this night must have awakened you, surely."

"You will soon see," said Buinne, hitching his swordbelt around him, "my father Fergus has not abandoned you, nor have we!"

"Now bring up grappling hooks and scaling ladders," shouted Concobar, and he sent men scrambling up the red log walls to break in through the high windows of the fortress. But this proved no difficulty to the defenders within, and the attackers were driven repeatedly from the narrow barred windows and ledges with great loss of life, for those who were not struck directly had their skulls cracked by the fall. All remained safe inside the Red Branch, but there was no time for rest or jubilation.

Next there began the low thunderous clout of a battering ram upon the heavy oak door. In the darkness and confusion Buinne Roughred was able to slip unseen from a window, and he leapt into the midst of the unarmed men working the ram, taking them totally by surprise, scattering their firebrands and torches, killing a dozen at his onrush, confounding the attackers with his mighty shout of doom.

Concobar, who could see nothing of the man but the torchlight upon his cloak, called out through the darkness, "Who is there bringing destruction on my men like this?"

"None other than Buinne the Roughred, the first and foremost son of Fergus macRoigh!" came the triumphant answer.

"Now Buinne," said the king, "there is no quarrel between ourselves. I will give you a good gift if you will leave off: a cantred of land, a place at my table, and the power of my word when it's needed. What do you say to that, Buinne?"

"Better a king's generosity than the favors of a widow," thought Buinne, and he said, "I'll take that gift!" So that was how he went over to the hand of Concobar. And it was a good and fruitful mountain he was given that night but not long afterwards a blight fell upon it, turning it to moorland—waste and profitless.

Deirdre overheard what had taken place, and with a bitter smile she said to Naisi, "By the moon and stars, Roughred Buinne has turned withershins and is gone over to the hand of the king. Now it makes me wonder if *both* sons of Fergus are nothing but their father's echo."

"Buinne is gone, but he did good work before he went," said Naisi, just as the harsh booming voice of the battering ram took up its earsplitting task anew.

"Too much more of that and they'll soon be in among us," shouted Illand Fairheaded. "I'll not desert your cause so long as I can lift this sword." And Illand leapt out and made a furious round of the Red Branch, the sparks flying from the edge of his weapon like fiery rain, bringing vicious slaughter upon the hireling troops.

"Call him out," said Concobar. "This will be as simple as the other." But Illand Fairheaded was a good son, for he never refused aid to anyone in need and he never accepted so much as a calf from anyone but Fergus.

"I claim the royal right of single combat in the name of Fergus macRoigh. My challenge to the household of Concobar macNessa!"

Basely the king called his own son Fiacra to him saying, "It was on the same night that you and Illand were born, and as he is using his father's weapons, so you will have mine: my shield, Ocean; dart, Victorious; my gapped spear, Slaughter; and my sword, Gorm Glas, the blue-green. Bear yourself manfully against the son of Fergus. You must surely defeat him or the Crown of Ulster will fall from our hands. The divine powers in these weapons will protect you."

Searching through the dim thickening darkness, Fiacra found the son of Fergus and they made a red-wounding attack upon each other as those watching on all sides sent up a sigh of deep despair while the din and harsh sounds of their struggle echoed round the woods and hills. Soon it was Illand who hard-pressed the son of Concobar and sent him sprawling. At that moment, Conall Cearnach, chief of the knights of the Red Branch, was approaching Emhain Macha in his chariot. He soon heard the mournful sighing of the crowds and the ringing crash of weapons against Ocean, the king's great shield. Conall steered his chariot through the crowd of onlookers to find the fight. In the dim light he believed Concobar himself was in great danger beneath the shield and from the mighty onslaught of this opponent he saw there was no time to waste. Instantly he plunged his spear between the shoulder blades of the unknown assailant. Mortally wounded, Illand looked up and cried, "Was it you, Conall? Evil work you've done, with the sons of Uisnach under my protection."

"What trick has Concobar been playing here?" screamed Conall. "He will not get his own son back alive for this!" And with one side twist of his long sword he lifted the head from Fiacra. Then Conall knelt beside the fading Illand, who called out to the sons of Uisnach to keep faith in Fergus, flung his weapons toward the Red Branch and died on the soft green lawn of Emhain Macha. In grief and rage Conall swiftly remounted his chariot and drove away from the battlefield at full gallop to report the king's treachery towards Fergus and the brotherhood of the Red Branch.

The sons of Uisnach were now left alone to face the onslaughts of Concobar's hired soldiers.

"Give me the woman!" called Concobar once more. "She will not be harmed. It is enough that the king pardons her and calls her to his table and bed!"

Deirdre looked at Naisi and said softly, "No man and woman have loved better. You were my company when the fires on the hilltops were put out and the stars were our friends only. Do you remember that first night in the woods? We lay on leaves, and looking up when the first gray dawn awoke the birds, saw leaves above us. You thought that I still slept and, bending down to kiss me on the eyes, found they were open. Bend and kiss me now, for it may be the last before our death."

Hearing no answer from within the hostel, Concobar ordered the final attack: "Set the Red Branch in the forest of flames! Should any come out of it, put them to the sword!" A wave of the king's men assaulted the Red Branch, sending great sheets of fire running up its timbers.

"He's destroying his own palace, his own kingdom!" shouted Naisi as a climbing drift of smoke burst into a scarlet tongue of flame before his eyes.

"Let's out and die, or break away if there is any chance in this darkness," said Deirdre. "We will be roasted here surely as pigeons in an oven."

The sons of Uisnach then made a close firm fence of their shields, putting Deirdre in their midst and came out and away from the blazing lodge. Slicing a path through a hedge of spears, they gave three great leaps over the ramparts of Emhain Macha, leaving their pursuers far behind. But on the next hillside they were forced to pause in their headlong flight to lie hidden among the tall ferns while they bound the worst of their wounds.

At this the king frantically summoned the ancient druid Cathbad to him, pleading, "If these three run wild again we will have a civil war to contend with. Stop them, druid, before there is such butchery done here that enemies from all sides will be drawn to Ulster in its weakness. I pledge that I will be no further danger to the sons of Uisnach but let them only make agreement with me."

"Your destiny is to live a great deal longer," the sad-eyed druid told Concobar. "I have no power to oppose this destiny but my heart is sore within me from the vision I have of it." Reluctantly Cathbad told the king to have his men build roaring brushwood fires below the hilltop where the sons of Uisnach and Deirdre were standing their

ground. And when the crackling flames were hot, the druid cast green hazel branches upon them, bringing forth dark billowing clouds of suffocating smoke. All was blotted from view and no man could rightly see the other, only dim choking figures emerging from the gloom or disappearing into it. And with this cloud the druid worked an enchantment upon the children of Uisnach for they thought themselves to be engulfed in a sea of thick, viscid waves, and they soon cast down their weapons and spread their arms abroad as if to swim. And that is how the sons of Uisnach were overwhelmed, and the mercenaries came and took them without a blow, seizing and binding them, and bringing them before Concobar.

The king called for the sons of Uisnach to be slain, but none of the Ulstermen would stir. A deep shame was rising in each of them. Eoghan, of Fermanagh was among those who had come to Emhain Macha to make alliance with Concobar, with whom his western clansmen long had been at enmity. As a first demonstration of loyalty it fell upon Eoghan to kill the children of Uisnach while Concobar macNessa looked on, guarded by his thirty warriors so that no one might approach him in revenge.

They stood on Emhain Macha's once green lawn, with Cathbad's oily cloud still hanging above them in the early morning air, shrouding the smooth hill so that neither the men guarding the bound brothers nor the women watching from the ramparts could be certain whether it was day or night.

"Kill me first," said Ardan. "Being youngest, I have fewer farewells than my brothers."

"Being youngest you should live the longer. I would be first," said Ainlle.

"You have my sword," said Naisi, "the gift of Mannan, son of Lir, and its stroke is swift and clean. Let the three of us be struck by it at once, so that none of us may see his brothers shamed."

It was agreed, and Eoghan handed the sword to his strong man, Maine Redhand who dealt the single blow, beheading the three sons of Uisnach instantly. And the Ulstermen gave three sorrowful shouts and cried aloud.

Their bodies lay side by side on the ground like three beautiful saplings destroyed by a blasting storm. Deirdre knelt beside them, lamenting and kissing them and showering them with her tears. Before long she was led away and made to stand beside Concobar, with Levarcham there to comfort her.

Concobar ordered his men to dig a grave, and at its foot they raised a standing stone with the name of Uisnach hewn upon its edge in the language of the trees, and their funeral games were performed. It was at this time the druid cursed Emhain Macha and the bloodline of Concobar macNessa to the end of race and time.

As to Fergus, he arrived on the following day and straightaway allied himself with Cormac Connloingas, Concobar's own son, and Dubthach, the Beetle of Ulster, each with his own troop. The anger of these men cannot be told. They collected followers from all sides until they numbered three thousand, and they gave crimson battle to Concobar's household on the ridges of the hill of Macha. With violence they ravaged and laid bare and scorched and wounded and Fergus put a fringe of fire around Emhain Macha to burn it. Thereafter they went from Ulster in rage and wrath across the border to Connacht where they gave allegiance to King Aillil and Queen Maeve in exchange for their hospitality. During their sixteen years of exile, Fergus and his followers continued to undermine Concobar's power, and Ulster continued to weaken and tremble at their hands. Not one single night passed without their vengeful forays, crossing the boundaries to devastate Concobar's land.

As to Deirdre, whose prophecy had come to pass, she was kept near Concobar in the household for a year after the slaying of the sons of Uisnach. And though it might be a small thing to raise her head from her knee or to make a laugh over her lip, she never did it during that space of time, nor could she take her fill of food or quiet sleep. When they sent musicians to her she would sing to them only of the life she had known in Alba:

"A blessing eastward to Alba from me.
Pleasant it was to be upon her soft green slopes
As they went freely searching in her glens.
Welcome their homeward chant upon her sunstruck
mountains.

"It was Naisi would kiss my lips
My first man and my sweetheart.
Modest Naisi would prepare
A cooking pit in the forest floor.

"When they brought down the fleet red deer in the chase,
When they skillfully speared the salmon of the sparkling
stream,
Joyful and proud were they
To find me looking on.

"Often when my feet grew weary
Wandering the hills and valleys to be with them,
Lightly would they bear me homeward
Upon the bed of their linked spears and shields.

"Though your melodies delight you,
My pipers and trumpeters,
I have known a sweeter sound,
The singing of the sons of Uisnach.

"The heavy wave roar of Naisi,
So lovely the ear might want it constantly,
Ardan's string bright performance;
Ainlle's humming towards his wild hut.

"Naisi's close cropped hair I loved;
His fine form—a tall tree.
Sorrowful it is not to arise
To greet the return of my husband.

"I loved this mighty warrior;
Loved his fitting, firm desire;
Loved him at daybreak as he dressed
By the edge of the wood.

"Beloved blue eyes which melted the women of Alba
And yet were so fierce towards adversaries.
And always, our forest journey done,
The warm reflection by the fireside.

"I take no joy in dressing;
I do not crimson my nails;
I have no welcome today for the pleasant speech of nobles,
Nor comfort in the fine houses of the king.

"There is no sleep for me now.
Half the night in my bed
My attention is flung on these ceaseless crowds.
All these long, long days."

As Concobar saw that neither games nor mildness profitted him, and that neither jesting nor exhaltation worked any change at all in her nature, he asked "Deirdre, who is it you hate most?"

"Yourself, surely," she said, "and Eoghan, the one who destroyed the beautiful children of Uisnach."

"Then you shall be a year on Eoghan's couch," said the king.

On the following morning they set out for the fair near Dundealgan. Deirdre was put behind Eoghan in the chariot and the king was riding along as well, to give her away at the bride's market. Deirdre kept her eyes toward the ground so she might not see the faces of the two men. Concobar looked at her and then at Eoghan and said, "Ah, Deirdre, it is the glance of a ewe set between two rams that you're giving us."

At these words she leapt up from the chariot and was gone, down the steep, rocky ledge beside the road. Concobar ordered the drivers to stop and set his men charging after the runaway girl. But all they found was her white body strewn upon the boulders and without life.

The king's men laid Deirdre's body in a separate grave near the palace, but during the night the people of the district took her body to rest in the grave of Naisi and his brothers. Concobar learned of this and had his men drive sharpened yew stakes through the corpses of the lovers to keep them apart. But the stakes soon sprouted, and by the turn of the year, two graceful yew trees were growing there side by side. Concobar had a firm warning from the druid to leave these trees

undisturbed and cease all persecution of the dead. The king went no further in the matter but turned his full attention to the war which was afterwards called the Cattle Raid of Cooley.

So ends the tragedy of the children of exile and the sorrows of Deirdre. "May the air bless her, and water and the wind, the sea, and all the hours of the sun and moon."

SOURCES AND GLOSSARY

SOURCES

Longes mac nUisnig (The Exile of the Sons of Uisnach). This story has existed by word of mouth since the 1st Century, A.D. and was written down by Irish scholars during the 7th Century, A.D. Senchan Torpeist, chief poet of Ireland during the 7th Century, A.D. was the first scholar who collected and wrote down fragments of the *Tain Bo Cuailgne* (The Cattle Raid of Cooley).

MANUSCRIPTS

The Book of Leinster (1151) Trinity College, Dublin

The Yellow Book of Lecan (1391) Trinity College, Dublin

The Glen Massan Manuscript (15th Century) Advocate's Library, Edinburgh

Edgerton Manuscript (1881) British Museum, London

ENGLISH LANGUAGE VERSIONS

The Tragical Fate of the Sons of Uisnech, Gaelic Society, Dublin, 1808

The Exile of the Children of Uisnech, Eugene O'Curry, Atlantis Magazine, Dublin, 1862

Deirdire, recited by John macNeill, translated by Alexander Carmichael, Club Leabhar, Ltd., Inverness, 1972

Lays of the Red Branch, Sir Samuel Ferguson, T.F. Unwin, 1897

The Fate of the Sons of Usnach, Lady Augusta Gregory, Putnam, 1902

Deirdre and the Sons of Usna, William Sharp, T.B. Mosher, 1903

The Death of the Sons of Uisnech, Ernst Windisch, Irische Texte, Leipzig, 1905

Deirdre, James Stephens, Macmillan, 1923

The Story of Deirdre, Vernam Hull, from *A Celtic Miscellany,* Penguin Classics, 1951

Irish Sagas and Folk Tales, Eileen O'Faolin, Oxford, 1954

Three Sorrowful Tales of Erin, F. M. Pilkington, Bodley Head, 1965

Deirdre, Madeleine Polland, Doubleday, 1967

The Tain, Thomas Kinsella, Oxford, 1969

PLAYS

Deirdre, William Butler Yeats

Deirdre of the Sorrows, John Millington Synge, Allen and Unwin

Deirdre, AE (George Russell)

BOOKS

Armagh County Guide, Armagh County Council; Nicholson & Bass Ltd., Belfast

The City of Armagh, Charles D. Trimble; Armagh Urban District Council

The Iron Age in the Irish Sea Province, Chas. Thomas, ed.; Council for British Archeology

A Concise History of Irish Art, Bruce Arnold; Praeger

Everyday Life of the Pagan Celts, Anne Ross; G. P. Putnam's Sons

A Celtic Miscellany, Denneth Hurlstone Jackson; Penguin Classics

Celtic Mythology, Proinsias macCana; Hamlyn

The Celts, T.G.E. Powell; Praeger

The White Goddess, Robert Graves; Noonday

The Emergence of Man: The Celts, Duncan Norton-Taylor; Time-Life Books

The Celts, Nora Chadwick; Penguin Books

Treasures of Ireland, A. T. Lucas; Viking

The Celtic Realms, Myles Dillon & Nora Chadwick; New American Library

Irish Art in the Early Christian Period, Francoise Henry; Methuen

Early Celtic Art, Paul Jacobsthal; Clarendon Press

Epic History of Ireland, James Standish O'Grady; Lemma

Literary History of Ireland, Douglas Hyde; T. F. Unwin

Celtic Art; The Methods of Construction, George Bain; Dover

Celtic Scotland, William Forbes Skene; Douglas

Scotland Before History, Stuart Piggott; T. Nelson

A Social History of Ancient Ireland and *The Story of Ancient Irish Civilization,* Patrick Weston Joyce; M. H. Gill & Son

TRAVEL LITERATURE

AA Illustrated Road Book of Ireland, The Automobile Association, Belfast

AA Illustrated Road Book of Scotland, The Automobile Association, London

Bartholomew's One-Inch and Half Inch Ordinance Survey Maps, Rand McNally, distributor

COLLECTIONS

The British Museum, London

The National Museum of Antiquities, Edinburgh

The National Museum, Dublin

The Armagh County Museum, Armagh

LIBRARIES

Stanford University, Palo Alto, California
University of California, Berkeley, California
University of British Columbia, Vancouver, B.C.

CREDITS

Page 14 "I see the flames of Emhain Macha . . ."
J. M. Synge, *Deirdre of the Sorrows*

Page 31 "I have heard he loves you as some old miser . . ."
W. B. Yeats, *Deirdre*

Page 86 "No man and woman have loved better . . ."
J. M. Synge, *Deirdre of the Sorrows*

"Do you remember that first night in the woods . . ."
W. B. Yeats, *Deirdre*

Page 104 "May the air bless her, and the water . . ."
J. M. Synge, *Deirdre of the Sorrows*

GLOSSARY

Ainlle (ANNla): "the handsome one"; the middle son of Uisnach.

Alba (AHLba): Britain, meaning England, Scotland and Wales. Specifically, in this story, the two Scottish highland districts of Argyll and Inverness.

Ardan (ARdan): "the proud one"; youngest son of Uisnach.

Argyll (ARgyll): "the Eastern Gael"; The seven centuries following this story witnessed a steady migration from Ulster to Scotland. Those remaining in Ulster referred to these emigrants as the Eastern Gael.

Armagh (arMAH): "the heights of Macha"; a crossroads since the Stone Age; a center of commerce, law, religion and learning. The city of Armagh is thirty seven miles southwest of Belfast.

Bay of Selma: now called Ardmucknish Bay, "height of the son of Naisi"; near the mouth of Loch Etive.

Belteine (BELteen): "festival of bonfires"; survives as May Day. Cattle were driven between bonfires as a protection against disease. Bridal fairs were held where marriage contracts of a year and a day were arranged.

Ben Edair (ben AYdir): the Hill of Howth, Dublin, east coast of Ireland.

Beorach (BOra): Commander of the seacliff fortress at Fair Head, County Antrim, Northern Ireland; overlooks the shortest waterway to Scotland.

Buinne (BWINye): Buinne Roughred, older son of Fergus.

Cathbad (CAHfa): high druid of Ulster. See Druid.

Cattle Raid of Cooley: see Tain bo Cuailgne.

Clanna Uisnach (CLAHna WISHna): Each of the three sons of Uisnach was head of a band of fifty clansmen, accompanied by families, menials and animals. Together they were known as the Clanna Uisnach.

Concobar macNessa (CONcobar, son of the Black Queen): high king of Ulster from 30 B.C. to A.D. 33. His mother married King Fergus of Ulster on the condition that Fergus abdicate in favor of young Concobar.

Connall Cernach (CONnal KEARney): veteran commander of the Red Branch; known as "the swift avenger."

Connacht (CONnat): the kingdom of the west, across the River Shannon. Connacht was the chief rival of the province of Ulster.

Cormac Conloingas (CORmac conLENas): "Cormac, leader of the exiles," Concobar's rebellious son.

Cuchulainn (kuhHOOlen): "the hound of the armorer," foremost hero of all the Red Branch Knights; stood off the armies of Connacht by defeating their champions in single combat for many days at a time when the rest of the Red Branch lay stricken by an epidemic. There is a bronze statue of Cuchulainn in the General Post Office, Dublin.

Deirdre (DAREdra): "One who gives warning." an older form, Derdriu, gives a meaning closer to "oak-prophet." The underlying theme of the story of Deirdre appears most anciently in the Sanskrit *Ramayana,* most famously in Homer's *Iliad,* and most distantly in Hawaiian legends.

Draighen (DRYhen): a freshwater beach on the Bay of Selma.

Druid (DREWid): reader of omens and portents; communicant with the other world; appeaser of the tribal deities; keeper of the calendar; tender of the sacred yew and rowan trees; chanter of spells and curses; professor. At public gatherings no one, including the king, was allowed to speak before the druid had spoken.

Dubthach (DUFfa): The Beetle of Ulster; named for the Irish black chafer beetle because of his bristling black eyebrows and his mastery of sarcasm and ridicule.

Dundealgan (doonDELga): the town of Dundalk, County Louth, Ireland.

Dun Fhada (doon FAHda): a hilltop in the Dalness Royal Forest, Glen Etive, Argyll.

Dun Fionn (doon FINN): a hilltop in the Dalness Royal Forest, Glen Etive, Argyll.

Dun macUisnach (doon mcWISHna): "stronghold of the sons of Uisnach"; also known as the hill of the armorers, and designated "Beregonium" on maps today. Parts of the fire-glazed walls survive on the ridge west of the hamlet of Ledaig, Argyll, overlooking the Bay of Selma.

Dun Sween: now called Castle Sween; on the southeastern shore of Loch Sween, Kilmory Knap, Argyll. An impressive twelfth century A.D. castle now stands on the massive natural rock foundation.

Elva (ELva): wife of Fedlimid the harper; Deirdre's natural mother.

Emhain Macha (EVan MAha): "the tracing of Macha," the fortress and shrine from which thirty-nine kings of Ulster ruled between 300 B.C. and A.D. 330, when invading armies covered it with nine feet of fresh earth.

Eoghan macDurthacht, king of Fermanagh (OWen mcDURtha, king of ferMANah): Fermanagh is the westernmost part of Ulster.

Erin (EHrin): Ireland. Three early princesses of Ireland (possibly 700 B.C.) were named Banba, Fola and Eireann.

Es-Ruaid (ESS ro): "the red cataract"; the salmon-leap at Ballyshannon, County Donegal, west coast of Ireland; a point on the ancient boundary between Ulster and Connacht.

Fedlimid macDall (FEHlimy): "son of the blind one"; harper to King Concobar; keeper of legends and genealogies; in modern terms, a musical historian.

Ferchertne (ferHAIRtin): Chief poet of Ulster. King Concobar was a patron of poets and an enthusiastic supporter of poets in training. Poets came from all over Erin to Emhain Macha in order to study and recite poetry.

Fergus, son of Roigh (Roy): "son of the great mare"; gave up the kingship of Ulster as a condition of marrying Nessa, who put her own young son, Concobar, on the throne. Fergus was famous as a poet and revolutionary general.

Five great fifths of Erin: The five provinces of Ireland; Ulster, Leinster, Munster, Connacht and Meath.

Gael (GAHL): "those keeping together"; relatives; countrymen; those who speak Celtic languages, especially the Irish, Highland Scots, Welsh, Cornish and Manx.

Glen Daruel (glen daRUel): "valley of the two roes" (red deer), its river flows southward into Loch Riddon, Southern Argyll.

Glen Etive (glen Ehtive): The windswept valley whose stream flows southwestward into Loch Etive. The upper reaches of the glen comprise the Dalness Royal Forest, Argyll.

Glen Loy: highland valley between Loch Argaig and Loch Eil, southern Inverness; its stream flows into Glen Mor, "the great glen."

Glen Massan (glen masSAHN): valley at the head of Holy Loch, five miles northwest of Dunoon, Argyll.

Glen Mor: "the great glen"; the rift valley of Scotland; a geologic fault forms a chain of long narrow lakes running straight northeast, dividing the Scottish mainland into two unequal portions.

Glen Orchy (Glen ORky): a broad valley whose river flows southwestward into Loch Awe, in Argyll.

Grianan Deirdre (GREENan DAREdra): "Deirdre's sunny bower"; designated on half-inch ordinance survey maps two miles east of Dalness, in Glen Etive, Scotland.

Hosting of Inverness: assembly of highland warrior clans, probably near the Stones of Clava, the burial ground of chiefs since 3500 B.C.; six miles east of the town of Inverness.

Illand (ILlan): Illand Fairhead, younger son of Fergus.

Island of the Thorn Bush (Inis Hail): Ancient burial island of Pictish chiefs, in the northeastern part of Loch Awe, Argyll.

King Aillil and Queen Maeve (AYElil and MAVE): rulers of the province of Connacht, western Ireland; Connacht was the chief rival of the province of Ulster.

Language of the trees, Ogham (OGam): The Celtic alphabet took its initials from the names of trees. The characters were chiseled on stone or notched in wood and read from the ground up.

Levarcham (LEVarcam): King Concobar's conversation-woman, satirist, poetess, news-reporter, Deirdre's adoptive mother.

Loch Etive (lock EHtiv): "the wild lake, lake of storms"; a narrow sea loch on the west coast of Scotland, north of the present city of Oban.

Loch Ness (lock NESS): "the black lake"; one of the long, deep lakes of Glen Mor; On its north shore, overlooking Urquhart, is a mountain named Carn Macsna, the hill of the sons of Uisnach.

Lough Neagh (loff NEEa): the largest body of water in Ireland; its flat shoreline is shared by five of the six counties of Ulster.

Lughnasa (lewNAsa): the festival of the August moon; Lugh is the Celtic god of light.

Mannan macLir (manAWN mcLEAR): son (or priest) of the Celtic god of the ocean.

The Moyle (mWILLa): the waters of the Irish Sea between Argyll, Scotland and County Antrim, Ireland, twelve miles apart.

Naisi (NEEsha): "the dark one"; the eldest son of Uisnach.

Palace of the King of Alba: speculatively Dunbarton, the rock fortress at the junction of the River Leven and the River Clyde, strategically important from the earliest times.

Rath: "a ring fort"; a farmstead; a small group of buildings enclosed by stone or timber defenses.

Rathlin Island: north of County Antrim, Ireland; a stepping stone between Scotland and Ireland.

Red Branch: the order of knighthood from which the kings of Ulster were chosen. These chariot warriors maintained hilltop fortresses in many strategic locations around Ulster, having their headquarters at the Inn of the Red Branch, upon the western approach to Emhain Macha.

Ridge of the Willows: site of the city of Armagh, County Armagh, Ireland.

Rudraighe (RUry): clan from which the high kings of Ulster were chosen.

Samhain (SAHven): a night of prophecy and magic where the correct rituals must be performed to pacify the supernatural forces which were believed to be at large at this season; survives as Halloween.

Sencha, son of Aillil (SENha, son of AYElil): the sergeant at arms of the order of the Red Branch; pacifier of disputes among its members; son of Aillil, the king of Connacht.

Sons of Uisnach (WISHna): Naisi, Ainlle, and Ardan; all knights of the Red Branch as was their father, Uisnach; They were trained as warriors in Scotland by their foster-mother, Scathach (SCOTta), then returned to their natural parents in Ulster at age 17. The custom of fosterage was a means of extending and strengthening the bonds of relationship between clan members and their neighbors.

Sunwise circles: clockwise circles; ritual form practiced by druids to shut out evil spirits.

Tain Bo Cuailnge (TAWN bo COOley): "the cattle raid of Cooley"; the oldest prose epic in Western literature; the collection of legends concerning the wars between the provinces of Ulster and Connacht during the first century, A.D. The Cooley Peninsula is north of Dundalk on the east coast of Ireland.

Uisnach (WISHna): married Indel, the daughter of Cathbad the Druid; She bore him three sons, Naisi, Ainlle and Ardan.

Ulster (ULLster): "land of the bearded ones"; In the days of this story the kingdom of Ulster spread across the present counties of Down, Antrim, and Armagh, in Northern Ireland.

Wood of Cuan (KWAHN): the south end of the island of Seil, connected by bridge to the coast of Argyll, ten miles south of Oban.

Barbara Lonigan